Paul Hoppe

BLOOMSBURY

NEW YORK BERLIN LONDON

New York • Berlin • London

To my mother

Published by Bloomsbury U.S.A. Children's Books, 175 Fifth Avenue, New York, New York 10010

Library of Congress Cataloging-in-Publication Data
Hoppe, Paul.
Hat / Paul Hoppe. – 1st U.S. ed.
p.   cm.
Summary: When Henry finds a hat, he is very excited by its possibilities but
becomes worried when he thinks that the hat might belong to someone else.
ISBN-13: 978-1-59990-247-0 • ISBN-10: 1-59990-247-8 (hardcover)
ISBN-13: 978-1-59990-248-7 • ISBN-10: 1-59990-248-6 (reinforced)
[1. Hats–Fiction. 2. Lost and found possessions–Fiction. 3. Imagination–Fiction.] I. Title.
PZ7.H77874Hat 2009   [E]–dc22   2008022357

Illustrations rendered with pen and brush using various inks on Arches Coldpress Watercolor Paper
Typeset in Bodoni Six Book • Book design by Donna Mark

First U.S. Edition 2009 • Printed in China by South China Printing
2 4 6 8 10 9 7 5 3 (hardcover)
2 4 6 8 10 9 7 5 3 1 (reinforced)

One day, Henry found a hat.

"Can I keep it?
Hat would be so cool!"

Hat protects from the sun.

Hat keeps off the rain.

Hat is great for catching mice

and performing
magic tricks.

Hat can be a boat, sailing far away,

or a sled, racing through the snow.

Hat saves Henry's life.

Hat makes Henry a star.

Hat makes Henry a *superstar*!

"But, Henry, what if someone else
needs this hat?"

A dancer in the spotlight.

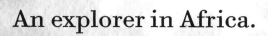

An explorer in Africa.

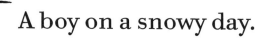

A boy on a snowy day.

A castaway on an island.

A magician
without tricks.

A terrified grandma!

A fancy girl dripping wet.

A lifeguard in the sun.

Henry thought about
every one of them . . .